The Colours We Eat

White Foods

Patricia Whitehouse

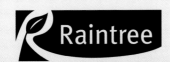
Raintree

www.raintreepublishers.co.uk
Visit our website to find out more information about **Raintree** books.

To order:
 Phone 44 (0) 1865 888112
📠 Send a fax to 44 (0) 1865 314091
💻 Visit the Raintree Bookshop at **www.raintreepublishers.co.uk** to browse our catalogue and order online.

First published in Great Britain by Raintree, Halley Court, Jordan Hill, Oxford OX2 8EJ, part of Harcourt Education.
Raintree is a registered trademark of Harcourt Education Ltd.

Editorial: Nick Hunter and Diyan Leake
Design: Sue Emerson (HL-US) and Joanna Sapwell (www.tipani.co.uk)
Picture Research: Amor Montes de Oca (HL-US) and Maria Joannou
Production: Jonathan Smith

Originated by Dot Gradations
Printed and bound in China by South China Printing Company

ISBN 1 844 21607 1
07 06 05 04 03
10 9 8 7 6 5 4 3 2 1

British Library Cataloguing in Publication Data
Whitehouse, Patricia
White Foods
641.3
A full catalogue record for this book is available from the British Library.

Acknowledgements
The publishers would like to thank the following for permission to reproduce photographs: Amor Montes de Oca p. **18**; Colour Pic, Inc. p. **23** (seed, E. R. Degginger); Craig Mitchelldyer Photography pp. **20**, **21**; Fraser Photos (Greg Beck) pp. **11**, **23** (kernels), back cover (popcorn); Gareth Boden pp. **15**, **23** (meringue); Heinemann Library (Michael Brosilow) pp. **1**, **4**, **5**, **6**, **7**, **8**, **9**, **10**, **12**, **13**, **14**, **15**, **16**, **17**, **19**, **22**, **23** (sprout), back cover (rice); Oxford Scientific Films p. **23** (leek).

Cover photograph of popcorn reproduced with permission of Heinemann Library (Michael Brosilow).

Every effort has been made to contact copyright holders of any material reproduced in this book. Any omissions will be rectified in subsequent printings if notice is given to the publishers.

 CAUTION: Children should be supervised by an adult when handling food and kitchen utensils.

Some words are shown in bold, **like this.** You can find them in the glossary on page 23.

Contents

Have you eaten white foods?

Colours are all around you.

How many different colours can you see in these foods?

All of these foods are white.

Which ones have you eaten?

What are some white foods?

Cauliflowers are white.

Have you ever eaten cauliflower cheese?

This loaf of bread is white.

It is made from white flour.

What are some white vegetables?

Turnips are white.

They are good to eat in soups and stews.

Onions can have white or brown skin.

We take off the skin and use the white part inside.

Have you tried these unusual white foods?

Bean sprouts are white.

They are **seeds** that have just **sprouted**.

Popcorn is easy to make.

When the **kernels** are hot, they pop and turn white.

Have you tried these other white foods?

White rice has to be cooked so it is soft enough to eat.

These eggs are white.

We can eat eggs in many ways.

Have you tried these crunchy white foods?

Macadamia nuts are crunchy and white.

They are the **seeds** of the macadamia tree.

Meringues are white and crunchy.

They are tasty to eat!

Have you tried these soft white foods?

Cottage cheese is soft and white.

It is made from milk.

Mashed potatoes are made with cooked potatoes.

They are soft and creamy!

What drinks and soups are white?

Milk is white.

Most milk we drink comes from cows.

Leek and potato soup is white.

It is made with **leeks**, potatoes and milk or cream.

Recipe: Creamy White Sundae

❗ Ask an adult to help you.

First, spoon vanilla yoghurt into a cup.

Sprinkle some coconut on the yoghurt.

Next, put in some whipped cream.

Add more layers until the cup is full.

Now, eat your creamy white sundae!

Quiz

Can you name these white foods?

Look for the answers on page 24.

Glossary

kernels
the small, yellow seeds
of sweetcorn

leek
a plant that looks like a
long onion

meringue
a sweet food made from
egg whites and sugar

seed
the part of a plant that grows
into another plant

sprout
grow from a seed

Index

Answers to quiz on page 22

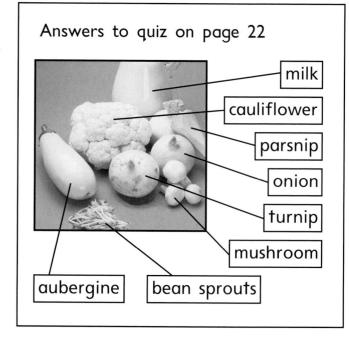

milk

cauliflower

parsnip

onion

turnip

mushroom

aubergine

bean sprouts

Titles in the Colours We Eat series include:

Hardback   1 844 21605 5

Hardback   1 844 21606 3

Hardback   1 844 21607 1

Hardback   1 844 21608 X

Hardback   1 844 21609 8

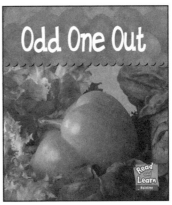

Hardback   1 844 21610 1

Find out about the other titles in this series on our website www.raintreepublishers.co.uk